I'm Not Very Good At It

Written by
Darrel Gregory

Illustrated
by Ari Miller

FriesenPress

Suite 300 - 990 Fort St
Victoria, BC, V8V 3K2
Canada

www.friesenpress.com

ISBN
978-1-5255-8097-0 (Hardcover)
978-1-5255-8098-7 (Paperback)
978-1-5255-8099-4 (eBook)

1. Juvenile Fiction, Social Issues,
Self-Esteem & Self-Reliance

Distributed to the trade by
The Ingram Book Company

For Genny and Vienna

Listen for dandelion seeds
landing on grass

My grandpa's birthday was a few days ago. My mom asked me if I would help make a *birthday card*.

My **brain** said,

"Okay, but I'm **NOT** very good at it."

The next day my mom asked me if I would help make a birthday cake.

My BRAIN said,

"Okay, but I'm **NOT** very good at it."

The next day my mom asked me if I would help make blueberry muffins for my preschool class.

My **BRAIN** said,

"Okay, but I'm **NOT** very good at it."

The next day my mom asked me if I would help build a birdhouse. My brain said,

"Okay, but I'm **DEFINITELY** not very good—"

"Now hold on a second," said my mom. "How come **every** time I ask you to help me with something, you tell me you're NOT VERY GOOD AT IT?"

"Because that's what my brain said," I said.

"Do you always listen to what your brain tells you?" asked my mom.

"Yeah, I guess," I said.

"Well, that's silly," said my mom.

"Who ELSE am I going to listen to?" I asked. "My big toe isn't going to tell me if I'm GOOD at something."

"How do you know?" said my mom. "Have you ever **TRIED** listening to your **big toe**?"

"No," I said. "I have **NEVER** tried listening to my big toe.

That's silly."

"You think so, do you?" said my mom. "What about your **OTHER** toes or your **NOSE** or your **EARS**? Have you ever tried listening to them?"

"No," I said. "I have never tried listening to my toes or my nose or my ears."

"I have **NEVER** tried listening to

my **TOES** or my **NOSE** or my **EARS.**"

"And what about your
HEART?" asked my mom.

"Have you ever tried listening
to your **HEART?**"

"I don't think so,"
I said.

"Maybe you should try it sometime," said my mom. "But there's a TRICK to listening to your heart.

It speaks very softly,
like dandelion seeds landing
on grass.

You must be still and quiet. Your **BRAIN** might try to BUTT in, but don't pay any attention to it. Your brain likes to make a lot of noise sometimes."

The next day my mom asked if I would help wash the car.

My **BRAIN** said,
"Okay, but I'm **NOT** very good at it."

The next day my mom asked me if I would help
plant some carrots in our garden.

My **BRAIN** said,
"Okay, but I'm **NOT**
very good at it."

This morning my mom asked me if I would help build a *model airplane.*

My **BRAIN** said,

"Okay, but I'm **NOT** very—"

"**Now hold on a second,**"
I said to my brain.
"**That's enough!**

You don't get to be the boss all the time. Right now I'm going to listen to my *big toe,* my *nose,* my *ears, **and** my heart.*"

I sat very still and quiet, like **DANDELION SEEDS** landing on grass.

I *listened* to my big toe and all of my other toes. I listened to my nose and my ears.

And I *listened* to my HEART.

Then I said to my brain,

"BRAIN, we decided that it doesn't matter if I'm **NOT** very good at something. We decided that the most important thing is *to just try.*"

At suppertime my mom said, "What if your brain tells you that you **DON'T LIKE** broccoli? Are you going to listen to it?"

"YES,"

I said.
"I know my brain is right about that.
I'm sure I don't like
BROCCOLI."

About the Author

Darrel Gregory was inspired to write this story after hearing his grand-daughter say "Okay, but I'm not very good at it." He hopes the book will help children to recognize at an early age that they don't always have to listen to the noise their brains make, and he hopes children will be invited to explore the possibility of trying regardless of the result.

Darrel lives in Edmonton, Alberta, with his two granddaughters nearby. I'm Not Very Good at It is his first children's book. He is currently working on his next book.

CPSIA information can be obtained
at www.ICGtesting.com
Printed in the USA
BVHW051650191220
596040BV00002B/25